2.8
1/2 pt.

# 5010 CALLING

### BY J. POWELL

illustrated by
Paul Savage

**Librarian Reviewer**
Joanne Bongaarts
Educational Consultant
MS in Library Media Education, Minnesota State University, Mankato
Teacher and Media Specialist with Edina Public Schools, MN, 1993–2000

**Reading Consultant**
Elizabeth Stedem
Educator/Consultant, Colorado Springs, CO
MA in Elementary Education, University of Denver, CO

**STONE ARCH BOOKS**
Minneapolis San Diego

First published in the United States in 2006
by Stone Arch Books,
151 Good Counsel Drive, P.O. Box 669,
Mankato, Minnesota 56002.
*www.stonearchbooks.com*

Originally published in Great Britain in 2005
by Badger Publishing Ltd.

Original work copyright © 2005 Badger Publishing Ltd
Text copyright © 2005 Jillian Powell

*Library of Congress Cataloging-in-Publication Data*
Powell, Jillian.
    5010 Calling / by J. Powell; illustrated by Paul Savage.
    p. cm.
    "Keystone Books."
    Summary: Zac gets into all sorts of trouble while thought-linked
to Beta, a boy living in the year 5010 who needs his help on a history
assignment.
    ISBN-13: 978-1-59889-012-9 (hardcover)
    ISBN-10: 1-59889-012-3 (hardcover)
    [1. Schools—Fiction. 2. Science fiction.] I. Title: Fifty ten calling.
II. Savage, Paul, 1971– ill. III. Title.
PZ7.P87755Aae 2006
[Fic]—dc22                                                    2005026334

1 2 3 4 5 6 11 10 09 08 07 06

# TABLE OF CONTENTS

## Chapter 1

# A HISTORY
# LESSON

"Good morning, Beta." A face appeared on the wall. It was Beta's history teacher.

"Today, you will begin your history project," said Beta's teacher. "It's on life in the year 2000."

"But that's 3,000 years ago!" Beta exclaimed.

"It's a history project."

"Yes, but that's so long ago!" Beta said. "I mean, there isn't much stuff about that time period, is there?"

The teacher's face vanished.

A movie came on. It showed people cheering. They were watching men kicking a ball back and forth.

"This is a game that was played in the year 2000. The players used their feet, so some people called it football," his teacher said. "Others called it soccer."

Another picture came on.

"This was called a dome," his teacher explained. "It was built in the year 2000."

"It looks like the bio-domes we live in," Beta said.

"Yes, but people didn't live in this dome," the teacher said. "People played sports there."

A new picture flashed on.

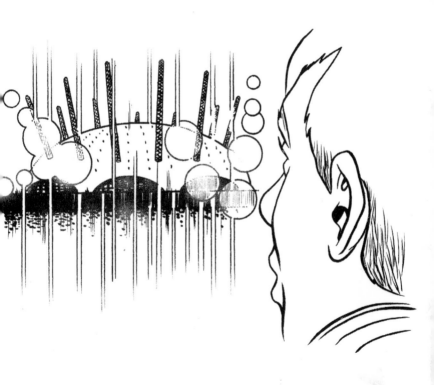

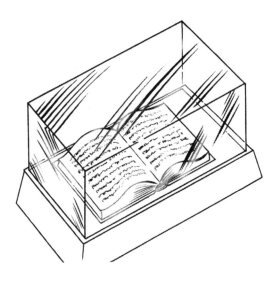

"What's that?" Beta asked.

"It's called a book," the teacher told him. "In the year 2000, people used books to get information. There are some books in our history museum."

"But this isn't much to go on for my project," Beta said.

"We are setting up a thought-link for you," the teacher said.

"You will have a thought-link with a boy named Zac. He is the same age as you," said the teacher. "He can tell you what life was like in the year 2000. Are you ready?"

## Chapter 2

# A BREAKFAST SURPRISE

"Hurry up, Zac. You'll be late for school," Mom said.

Zac was just finishing his breakfast.

"Okay, I'm going," he said. Zac was grumpy in the morning.

"Where are you going?" a voice asked inside Zac's head. It was Beta.

"I'm going to school," Zac said aloud. He was still half asleep.

"Well, go then!" Mom said. "And don't forget your soccer equipment."

"Soccer! You play soccer!" Beta exclaimed in Zac's head.

"What was that?" Zac asked.

"I said, don't forget your soccer equipment," Mom repeated.

"No, not that —" said Zac.

"It's me, Beta," Beta said. "Calling you from the year 5010. Can you hear me, Zac?"

"I can hear you!" Zac exclaimed.

"Well, what are you waiting for!" Mom said. "Just go, Zac. You're going to be late!"

"I have to go," Zac said to Beta.

"That's okay," Beta replied. "I'm coming with you!"

## Chapter 3

# BETA COMES TOO

"Look, who did you say you were?" Zac asked.

It was strange talking to someone he couldn't see, and nobody else could hear.

"My name is Beta. I am a boy the same age as you. That's why they chose you for my thought-link."

"What's a thought-link?" Zac asked.

"It's what we are doing now," Beta explained. "We have a link, so you can hear me in your thoughts. I can hear what you say, too. I am doing this project, you see. It's on life in the year 2000. I need you to tell me all about it."

"That's weird!" Zac said. He was about to ask something else when he saw Ben and Jordan.

"Talking to yourself, Wacky Zacky?" Jordan said. "That's the first sign that you're going crazy!"

"I'm just reviewing," Zac replied. "You know, for the I.T. test."

"What's I.T.?" Beta chipped in.

"Information Technology," Zac said.

"Yeah, we know what I.T. is," Jordan said, giving Zac an odd look.

"Ah! I heard you had computers with screens, and you had to use your fingers to work with them," Beta said.

"Don't you have I.T. anymore?" Zac asked. He forgot about Ben and Jordan. Beta was making computers sound like antiques!

"What are you talking about?" Ben asked. "We're all taking the I.T. test this morning. You're losing it, Zac!"

They had arrived at the school gates. Ben and Jordan went in, giving Zac an odd look.

## Chapter 4

# TROUBLE WITH
# BETA

Beta asked Zac questions at the worst times. Zac got into trouble for talking during assembly.

"If you can't behave, maybe you should stay in at lunchtime," Zac's teacher told him.

"Do you mind having to go to a school everyday?" Beta chipped in.

"Doesn't bother me," Zac said. Then he realized what he had said. His teacher looked at him and scowled.

"Really? Then you better stay in during afternoon break, too!" said his teacher.

Zac spent both breaks answering Beta's questions.

"What are stores?" Beta asked.

"Places where you buy stuff," Zac told him.

"You mean you have to go out to get things you need?" Beta made it sound crazy.

"Well, you can order some stuff on the Internet, but yes. People like shopping," Zac told him. "I'm going shopping on Saturday. I'll tell you about it then."

Zac needed some new sneakers. On Saturday morning, he went to his favorite store.

"I need you to tell me what the store is like," Beta told Zac.

"We're in the sporting goods department," Zac said. "There's some great stuff here! Tell you what, I'll take a few pictures with my cell phone. That might help you."

Zac started snapping.

"Okay, we'll start with some new sportswear," he told Beta.

Suddenly, Zac felt a tap on his shoulder.

"I think you'd better come with me, young man," a voice said.

## Chapter 5

# A LUCKY BREAK

"It's no good," Zac told Beta later. "You'll have to find someone else. You're getting me into trouble. They thought I was shoplifting!"

"Shoplifting?" Beta asked.

"Taking stuff from the store," said Zac. "And it didn't help when I told them I was talking to you in 5010."

"I thought they were going to call for a doctor," continued Zac.

"A doctor? I heard you sometimes needed body repairs," Beta said.

"Don't you have enough for your project now?" Zac asked.

"But you were going to tell me about these . . . sneakers. Things you put on your feet," said Beta.

"It's a strange idea to us," Beta continued. "Our feet have a microchip inside that adapts them to the ground. We can set them for soft or hard ground, or even for snow."

"Okay, look! I do need to get some shoes," Zac told him. "But after that, I'm calling it a day, okay?"

Zac went to the new sporting goods store in town. He had seen some amazing new shoes there. "These are just so cool," he told Beta.

"Cool? You mean they keep your feet from getting too hot?" Beta asked.

"No, I mean they're like . . . really cool," Zac said.

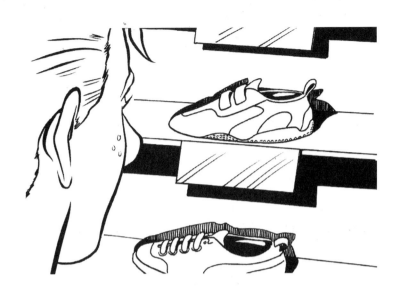

"You've heard of street cred?" Zac asked. "These shoes give you feet cred!"

"Hey, that's great!" a voice chipped in. This time it wasn't Beta. It was a man standing right behind Zac.

"I'm the advertising brains for this brand," the man told Zac. "That's a great slogan you've come up with!"

"In fact," the man continued, "your face would be great for our new ads. I'll give you my card. Give my office a call, okay?"

Zac took the card, ignoring Beta's non-stop questions. Things were looking up!

## Chapter 6

# LOGGING OFF

The next day, Zac told Beta, "I'm going to be on television!"

"Television? They were boxes with screens, like your computers, right?" Beta asked.

"Well, we do have plasma screens," Zac said.

Sometimes Beta made the year 2000 sound like the Stone Age!

"Well, I have some good news, too," Beta said. "I got a perfect score on my history project, thanks to you!"

"Great!" Zac exclaimed.

"Now I have to help someone else," Beta told Zac. "I am having a thought-link with a boy from the year 8000. He is doing a history project on life in my time."

"Now that's weird," Zac said.

"So it's time for me to log off and wish you luck!" Beta said.

"Okay!" Zac said. In a funny sort of way he was going to miss Beta. "Good luck, too, and say hi to the guy in 8000 for me!"

It must be nice having a thought-link whenever you need help, Zac thought. No one was going to help *him* with his project on the Romans . . .

## Chapter 7

# HEARING VOICES

The next day, Zac went to the museum to work on his report for school. The museum had several rooms on the Romans.

He took a notebook and paid for one of the headsets that told you about the things in each room.

Some of the rooms were filled with statues and vases.

There were also some paintings of faces — a woman, a man, and a boy.

"This is a painting of a boy who lived nearly 2,000 years ago," the headset told him.

"He's about 12 years old," said the headset. "He was probably . . ."

"Hello!" said a strange new voice from inside Zac's head.

Zac was confused and played the tape back on the headset.

"This is a painting of a boy who lived nearly 2,000 years ago. He's about . . ."

"I said hello!" the other voice cut in again.

Zac took off the headset.

He turned it off and stared at the painting of the boy.

"Hi, Zac," a boy's voice said inside Zac's head.

# ABOUT THE AUTHOR

Jillian Powell started writing when she was very young. She loved having a giant pad of paper and some pens or crayons in front of her. She made up newspaper stories about jewel thieves and spies. Jillian's parents still have her early stories, complete with crayon illustrations!

# ABOUT THE ILLUSTRATOR

Paul Savage works in a design studio, drawing pictures for advertising. He says illustrating books is "the best job." He's always been interested in illustrating books, and he loves reading. Paul also enjoys playing sports and running.

He lives in England with his wife and daughter, Amelia.

# GLOSSARY

**bio-dome** (BYE-oh DOHM)—a large living area that is covered with a dome to protect those living inside

**cred** (KRED)—short for credibility; something you can believe is true.

**microchip** (MYE-kroh-chip)—a small piece of electronic equipment used to store information

**shoplift** (SHOP-lift)—to take something from a store without paying for it

**slogan** (SLOH-guhn)—a phrase or motto used by a business in advertising; a slogan is usually used to attract customers.

**thought-link** (THAWT-LINGK)—a connection to someone else's thoughts; thought-links are not real but are an idea of the future.

# DISCUSSION QUESTIONS

1. Beta lives in a bio-dome. What do you think life in a bio-dome would be like? Why do you think people might need to live inside bio-domes in the future?

2. When Beta's history class begins, the teacher's face simply shows up on the wall. Beta does not sit in a classroom or study books. Do you think you would learn better if today's schools were more like Beta's school? Or do you think you learn best in classrooms? Why?

3. At the beginning of the story, Beta says that nothing interesting could have happened 3,000 years ago. By the end of the story, how has Beta's opinion about the year 2000 changed?

# WRITING PROMPTS

1. If Beta contacted you, write about the things you would show him from your life.

2. If you could create a thought-link with someone from the past, who would you like to contact? Write about why you chose this person.

3. Beta tells us a few things about the year 5010. There are no shopping malls, no doctors, and no tennis shoes. Write about other ways you think the world might be different 3,000 years from now.

# ALSO BY
# J. POWELL

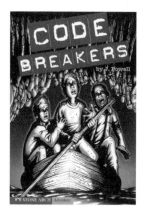

### Code Breakers
1-59889-010-7

*One ordinary afternoon, three friends find a strange briefcase on a park bench. Discover the danger and adventure that await them as the boys decide to follow the mysterious clues they find inside the case.*

### Webcam Scam
1-59889-011-5

*Carl's family is thrilled when they are chosen for a reality Web show. But Carl has his doubts. When it seems that there is more to it than meets the eye, Carl has to act.*

# OTHER BOOKS
# IN THIS SET

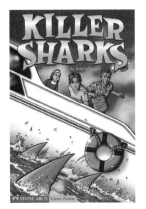

### Killer Sharks
*by Stan Cullimore*
1-59889-013-1

*The Brown family is relaxing on their speedboat when, suddenly, deadly sharks surround them — but these are no ordinary sharks. Who sent the killer sharks? And will the Browns get out alive?*

### Terror World
*by Tony Norman*
1-59889-008-5

*Jimmy and Seb love playing the games at Terror World arcade. When the owner offers them a free trial of a new game, they enter the real "Terror World." Chased by razor cats, it seems they have no escape.*

# INTERNET SITES

Do you want to know more about subjects related to this book? Or are you interested in learning about other topics? Then check out FactHound, a fun, easy way to find Internet sites.

Our investigative staff has already sniffed out great sites for you!

Here's how to use FactHound:

1. Visit *www.facthound.com*

2. Select your grade level.

3. To learn more about subjects related to this book, type in the book's ISBN number: **1598890123**.

4. Click the **Fetch It** button.

FactHound will fetch the best Internet sites for you!